I WISH, I WISH

I wish   I wish

by LISL WEIL

Houghton Mifflin Company  19 57 Boston

PUBLISHED BY HOUGHTON MIFFLIN COMPANY, DISTRIBUTED TO THE
SCHOOLS BY XEROX EDUCATION PUBLICATIONS

LIBRARY OF CONGRESS CATALOGUE CARD NUMBER: 57-5881

THE RIVERSIDE PRESS
CAMBRIDGE · MASSACHUSETTS
PRINTED IN THE U.S.A.

To Francesca's Godmother

I WISH, I WISH

Along the banks of the river Arno in Italy, there is an old-world city, full of splendor. With its golden towers and many palaces, it looks like a real fairy land.

In this beautiful city of Florence lives little Francesca.

Francesca does not live in a palace with rich treasures.
She lives in a narrow house
in a narrow street
with her mamma and papa and brother Nino.

Sometimes Francesca and Nino play hide and seek with the other children.

Sometimes Francesca chases a butterfly all by herself.

But, most of all, Francesca likes to go to the Galleria
Pitti. Here among the beautiful paintings in gold frames —
some large, some small —
Francesca dreams about a wish that is close to her heart.

It is a secret wish.

Many artists from all over the world come to the Galleria to make copies of the great masterpieces.

The smallest pictures of all are painted by an American
lady. Francesca never tires of watching the lady hidden
under a big hat. And never, never does she get too close to
the lady for fear of disturbing her.

But to herself, Francesca whispers over and over again,

"Oh, I WISH

I could have a painting all my own —

just a little one to take home."

Even when Francesca helps her mamma weave baskets, her thoughts are always on her wish.

One day when Francesca was on her way to the Galleria, thinking her secret thoughts, she suddenly tripped over a cat.

"Excuse me," she said — and went on.

The cat followed her and kept getting between her
feet all the time. Finally Francesca stopped and bent down.
Around the cat's neck was a locket on a chain.

Now, there are lots and lots of cats in Florence. But Francesca had never seen one wearing a locket.

On the locket was a picture of a lady.

"You lovely cat," Francesca said. "You must go home to your mistress — go — go." And she sent the cat off with a gentle push.

As usual, Francesca stayed so long in the Galleria that
Nino had to come and fetch her.

When they left, they did not see the cat
sleeping on the steps, waiting . . .

Later, that night, Francesca heard a sad cry out in the narrow street. She went to the window and in the dark below was the strange cat, meowing and meowing.

Francesca just had to let her in.

And the next morning, there were two cats in the basket.

Nino no longer had to call for Francesca at the Galleria. Every day she went to watch the American lady but she always remembered to come home early so that she could play with the cats.

And before long, the kitten's eyes were open and she was bouncing around after Francesca like a ball of snow-white fur.

"Oh, I WISH, I WISH

you belonged to me, you sweet little kitten."

"No, no," said Mamma and Papa, shaking their heads.

"The cat belongs to the lady on the locket, and now the kitten belongs to her, too.

"You must try to find the lady — that's the right thing to do."

Francesca knew she must do the right thing but she said to herself: "I do *not* wish to find the mistress of the kitten.

"But I will try . . .

I will."

The Sisters said, "No, we have never seen this lady."

The man on the wine cart said, "No. I don't know her."

The Flower lady said,
"What a pity."

The soldiers just shook their heads.

"Let me see
the picture on the locket," said the cobbler.

Everyone at the market knew Francesca but nobody
knew the lady.

Signore Tucci who sells birds said, "You had better ask the officer, Francesca."

The policeman had heard nothing of lost cats.

Francesca's heart leaped.
Maybe she could keep the
lovely cats after all.

She had tried, hadn't she?

She would take them home now.
That's what she would do.

The next morning, Francesca hugged the kitten goodbye, patted the cat and then ran breathlessly to the Galleria.

She had missed a whole day.

What if the American lady had gone and taken her little pictures away?

No. The lady was there.

Francesca crept slowly and softly toward the lady.

Suddenly there was a great commotion at the entrance to the Galleria.

The lady turned . . . Francesca gasped . . .

There were the guards racing about trying to catch the cat and the kitten.

They had followed Francesca!

And cats were not permitted in the Galleria.

The cat sprang right up into the lady's lap.

The kitten licked Francesca's ankle with her rough little tongue.

It was glorious reunion.

Only Francesca was a little sad. She was going to miss the little kitten.

When the lady could catch her breath, she said to the guard, "We'll take them out at once." And to Francesca, she said, "You have made me very happy. Will you help me carry the cats home?"

Francesca followed the lady to the big Hotel.

Up the elevator.

Into the lady's room.

Everything began to happen so quickly that Francesca
had to squeeze herself to be sure she was not dreaming.

The lady went over to her easel saying, "A little
kitten should belong to a little girl. And in case you lose
her . . . "

And that's how Francesca's wishes both came true.
It was just like a real fairy tale.

With her very own picture
and her very own
kitten Francesca
felt like a fairy tale
Princess

As she skipped happily home
To her narrow house

In the narrow street
In the real city of Florence